MW01105490

Anna

and the Earth Angel

written by Stephanie Hrehirchuk

illustrated by Joy Bickell

cover art by Stephanie Hrehirchuk

Every print copy sold plants a tree.
Follow the growth of Anna's forest at
www.createyourforest.ca/visit/annas-forest

Anna and the Earth Angel

Published by Anna's Angels Press

Anna and the Earth Angel, Stephanie Hrehirchuk

Copyright © 2017 by Stephanie Hrehirchuk

Copy editor: John Breeze
Consulting editor: Maraya Loza Koxahn
Illustrations: Joy Bickell
Cover art: Stephanie Hrehirchuk
Interior design: Robyn Monkman

Printed and bound in Canada by Blitzprint, Calgary

ISBN 978-0-9958839-0-1

Printed on recycled paper.

For Scott,
Matthew
and Kasha

"BORED," said Anna to the ceiling. "B-O-R-E-D. Bored. I'm bored. Borrrrrrrrrrrrrrrrrrrrrred." She used her whole breath on that one word.

Anna's family had just moved to a new neighborhood. Anna didn't know anyone in this new place. She had no idea what she'd do with her long summer days without school.

"Go outside and make some new friends, Anna," said her mom cheerfully from behind a large packing box in the kitchen.

"Go check out the playground," added her father on his way upstairs, carrying Anna's baby sister. "There are bound to be kids there."

Anna missed her old friends. She missed jumping on Kyla's trampoline. She missed helping Leila walk her dog named Charlie.

Charlie was a pug and snorted while he walked, which made Leila and Anna laugh. Anna missed her doorbell ringing. No one rang Anna's doorbell at the new house to invite her out to play.

Anna saw nothing special about this new neighborhood. There were sidewalks and playgrounds, and a tree in every front yard. People walked their dogs. Some dogs walked their people. To Anna it looked a lot like her old neighborhood, except without her friends.

Anna stretched out sideways across the big brown leather chair in the corner of the living room, with her head on one armrest and her legs flopped over the other. She stared at the ceiling. Then she looked out the large window at the seemingly endless blue sky. She could see the mountains in the distance, the trees across the valley and the pond down below. Suddenly, she shot up straight and stared out the window.

"There's a *pond* here?" she excitedly asked her black cat, George, who was napping on the back of the chair. George opened one eye, licked his paw and rubbed it over his closed eye. Then he closed the other eye.

"Well *you* might not find it interesting, George, but I'm going down there," said Anna. "I'm going to explore the pond."

Anna jumped off the chair, slipped into her shoes and headed out the front door before George could reply.

"Mew," he said to an empty room and went back to sleep.

Anna followed a paved path along the ridge behind her house. Looking down the grassy hill, she spotted the pond on the other side of the road. But the paved path didn't go there. Anna wondered how to get to the pond. Suddenly, she spied a well-trodden trail through the tall grass.

"This must be a neighborhood shortcut," she said to herself, and trotted down the trail toward the road. At the road, she found a sidewalk. Near the sidewalk, she found a crosswalk. Anna looked right, then left, then right again; then she looked left, right and left again. She made super sure the road was clear before she darted across the empty lanes and arrived at the other side. Anna stopped and stared wide-eyed at the pond.

Another grassy trail led Anna from the road to a gravel walking path that looped around the pond. Young trees sprouted up like a natural fence, separating the pond from the road. As Anna neared the pond she saw several kinds of ducks. Some were black and white. Others had shiny green heads on brown bodies. Two large geese glided along the water.

"HONK!" sounded the larger goose as Anna approached.

"Well, honk to you, too," Anna replied.

Suddenly, a bird darted at her head. She ducked. The bird landed on the high branch of a nearby tree and gave a shrill call as if scolding her.

"Well that's no way to welcome someone," she scolded the bird right back. Anna could see that the shiny black bird had a red patch on each wing.

"You're a red-winged blackbird!" she exclaimed. "I read about you in school. I'm so pleased to meet you. Don't worry, I won't disturb your nest." The bird gave a shrill reply and flew off into the cattails along the pond's edge.

Anna continued on the path. She saw wild roses in pinks and whites, small green plants loaded with tiny blue flowers, and creeping vines with yellow and orange blossoms. Anna took care not to step on the delicate flora.

"What a wonderful place this is!" Anna cheered, as she continued around the pond.

Next, she came to three big trees. Two wide trees with many twisting trunks grew on one side of the path. One taller tree with sky-reaching branches and narrow trunk grew on the other side of the path. These three trees formed a gateway to the pond.

Seeing that they were the largest and oldest trees in the area, Anna paused to greet them. She bowed to them, saying, "Permission to pass, please." She smiled as she imagined the trees nodding at her in approval. Laughing out loud, she continued on her way. Anna walked the full loop around the pond before returning home, thrilled by her new discovery.

"The pond is amazing," Anna told her parents.

"It's called Two-Toed Pond," replied her mom while spreading egg salad onto bread for sandwiches.

"Two-Toed Pond?" asked Anna. "Why Two-Toed?"

"If you look at it from up high," replied her dad, clearing moving boxes off the table for lunch, "the pond has a little island running partway down the middle, splitting the upper part of the pond in two. It looks kind of like a deer's hoof that is split into two toes."

"Two-Toed Pond," repeated Anna. "I like that."

That summer, Anna went to Two-Toed Pond every day. She always triple-checked the road for traffic. She always greeted the red-winged blackbird, who always greeted her first, and she always bowed to the guardians of the pond, the three big trees.

One day, as she was walking along the gravel path, Anna paused at the far end of the pond. She looked up the hillside beyond and wondered what might be there. She had never ventured farther than the pond's path. This day, however, she felt strangely pulled from the path, so up the grassy hillside she went.

By the time she reached the top of the hill, Anna was huffing and puffing. She bent over to catch her breath, hands on her knees. Looking down at her feet she saw bluebells. No, not bluebells. Anna remembered that the wild ones were called harebells. The flowers looked so delicate, with their small bells in shades of blue. There weren't any harebells down by the pond.

Then she saw brown-eyed Susans: large, orange flowers with a dark center that looked like a big eye. There weren't any brown-eyed Susans near the pond either. This area was very different from the pond.

Anna stood up. She could see for miles. From the top of the hill she could see the next hill and the next, with the river playing hide-and-seek between the hills. The mountains looked closer and the air tasted sweeter. Anna closed her eyes and took in a deep breath.

When she opened her eyes again, she noticed a grove of trees on the other side of the flowery hilltop. Anna headed for it.

Along the way, she paused at an old farm fence that stood between her and the trees. The barbed wire was missing from one section. The opening allowed Anna access to the tiny forest. Remembering her tree gate below and her manners, Anna once again bowed.

"Permission to enter?" she requested. But Anna didn't laugh aloud like she had when she first bowed to the three trees. Anna felt different in this place. She felt calm and quiet and respectful.

Anna found a log to sit on. She watched butterflies flit from flower to flower. She spotted ladybugs on the long grasses. A tiny, thin-legged gold spider crawled up her ankle. She invited it onto her finger and placed it back on the grass. She watched the tiniest ants march across a patch of dirt in single file, no ant out of order.

Anna decided that this would be her special place. Her very own sacred space. Everything in it seemed to welcome her, from the gold thin-legged spiders to the dancing orange butterflies and the pale blue harebells.

Anna loved her special place. She returned often during her summer break. Some days she sat on the ground and enjoyed the company of the creepy crawlies and the harebells nodding agreeably in the breeze. On other days she brought her journal and pencil and sketched the brown-eyed Susans and butterflies. Sometimes she wrote poems or jotted down ideas that drifted through her head like the clouds through the blue sky above her.

Some days she saw deer on the hill. Some days the wandering coyotes saw Anna on the hill and she watched them trot quickly back into the valley. Once she completely lost track of time, mesmerized by the sun setting over the mountains in the west and turning the whole sky pink, while the full moon rose over the city skyscrapers in the east.

Anna's special place was indeed a magical place, though Anna had no idea just how special her special place was. For deep inside the hill an earth angel lay sleeping, waiting for the right time to awake.

Anna told no one of her special place, not even her cat George, although he would probably keep her secret. After all, cats are good at keeping secrets. But this place was too special to share, even with George.

Summer holidays ended and school began again. Anna got busy with new classes, new friends and new teachers. Anna had no time to visit her special place. Winter came and went.

"Today we will learn about prairie crocuses," said Mrs. Hewitt, Anna's Homeroom teacher. "Crocuses are unique flowers. They are the first of the prairie flowers to bloom in spring, even through the snow. Their green leaves, purple blossom and yellow center provide welcome color after the white of winter. Although they are the first to flower, the blossoms only last a couple weeks. Then you must wait a whole year to see them again."

Anna loved learning about flowers. She liked to spot them when she went hiking in the mountains with her family. But Anna didn't have to wait to go hiking in order to find new flowers. Now she had a whole hillside of nature outside her back door.

Anna was excited to go looking for crocuses. Suddenly she thought of her special place. Anna wondered if crocuses grew there, so as soon as school was over that day, she headed outside in search of the purple flowers.

She found none at the pond. Anna headed up the hillside, keeping the image of her treasure clear in her mind. Anna's eyes stayed glued to the ground as she walked. Grass. Grass. More grass. Dense, heavy, matted grass. Thick prairie grass, weighed down from the season of snow. A winter-woven carpet of grass.

And suddenly – success – Anna spotted her first crocus! One small, purple petal peeked out from beneath a thick mass of grass. Anna was delighted. She continued up the hill. Another peeking petal, then a whole bloom, then bunches of blooms. Anna had hit the prairie crocus jackpot! Grinning from ear to ear, Anna followed the floral trail up the hill.

But at her special place, Anna found something that she didn't like. Didn't like at all! New houses were being built behind the little grove of trees. Big houses. Fancy houses.

Anna's heart sank. She felt sad returning to her special place and finding it filled with noisy construction and building materials stacked nearby. Now she couldn't sit and enjoy the silence. She couldn't write or sketch. And surely the deer and coyotes wouldn't come.

Anna stared at the stacked lumber behind the trees. She traced the mesh construction fence with her eyes, studying the perimeter of the building site. Bright blue flags clearly marked the boundaries of the buildings. The fence and the flags came no farther than the other side of the tiny forest. Anna felt certain that her special place would be safe from harm. Nevertheless, she decided not to return until the construction was complete. She bowed at the opening in the barbed wire fence and left.

That summer, Anna continued to visit Two-Toed Pond, but she never ventured up the hill to her special place. She would pause at the back of the pond and stretch her neck to look up the hillside, but couldn't see the tiny forest from her place on the path.

Fall soon returned and classes resumed. It was October and an unseasonably warm day. Anna decided it was time to visit her special place. She couldn't wait to get there. She selected her favorite rock from her collection as a gift. Anna set off around the pond, bowing, as was her custom, to the trees, who seemed to happily bow back at her, as if they knew she was headed for a reunion with her special place. Then she climbed up the hill to the entrance in the barbed wire fence.

What Anna saw there made her drop her rock. Her heart fell with it. Her special place had changed, but not from the construction. There were dirt trails where flowers once grew — trails carved deep into the earth. The logs she once sat on while she sketched were now ramps. While Anna had been away from the hilltop, someone had turned her special place into a bike course!

Anna began to cry. "Why would someone destroy such a wonderful place?" Anna sobbed. "Can't they see the magic?" She picked up her rock and walked along the dirt trail, looking for harebells through her tears.

Finally, something blue caught her eye. She walked toward it, to the edge of the hilltop, filled with sadness and a heavy heart. Amidst the tall, dry, wild grasses, one weathered blue bloom hung its head low on its stem, looking as sad as Anna felt. She leaned down to see it better. To Anna's surprise, next to the harebell she found a magnificent crocus, bursting through the thick dry grass.

Anna couldn't believe her eyes. She wiped away her tears and looked again.

"Yes!" she yelled out loud. "A crocus!"

Anna hadn't known if it was even possible for a crocus to bloom in fall. Suddenly she was filled with hope at the courage of the little flower.

"If you can find a way to bloom in fall," said Anna, "then I can find a way to believe *anything* is possible, including cleaning up this mess." She held her favorite rock in both hands and, smiling a big smile, she squeezed all her gratitude into the rock and placed it next to the little crocus.

"Thank you," she said.

Then something remarkable happened. The splendid being who had been sleeping inside the hill for many, many years, suddenly emerged from the earth. First, Anna saw her great wings. Then she saw her body. And finally, she saw her legs.

Anna's mouth fell open and she stared at this incredible sight.

"Who are you?" Anna finally found her words.

"I am an earth angel," replied the beautiful being.

The earth angel sat atop the hill with Anna. She was very tall, almost as tall as Anna's house. Her wings were bigger than her body. She folded her arms around her bent knees, hugging them into her chest and warming herself in the sun.

"Where did you come from?" continued Anna, still amazed by the sight of the earth angel.

"I live here," replied the earth angel. "I used

to spend my days on this hill, talking with the animals, the trees and flowers, and the people who would come to visit us. But the people stopped talking to the trees and listening to the wind. They stopped dancing with the animals and laughing with the flowers. They stopped coming. So I went to sleep inside my hill. Then your blessing today woke me."

Anna looked at the earth angel. The earth angel looked at the damage to her hilltop. Anna could see that the earth angel was sad.

"I'm so sorry," said Anna. "Someone has damaged this special place." Anna didn't know what else to say, so she and the earth angel sat silently overlooking the hillside as the sky grew dark.

"I have to go home now," said Anna. "But I'll come back tomorrow." The earth angel gave her a gentle smile and Anna went home.

That night, Anna lay in bed, her arms folded behind her head, staring out her window at the stars and thinking about the earth angel. The earth angel lay at the top of the hill on her grassy bed, her wings folded behind her head, staring at the stars and thinking about Anna.

The next day Anna went to school with a mission. She asked every kid in her class if they knew who built the bike trail. Dillon said he heard Lucas talking about the bike trail. Lucas said he heard Danica talking about the bike trail. Danica said Pria and Alexander had built the bike trail.

Anna told Pria and Alexander about the earth angel and that they had messed up her hill. Pria and Alexander laughed at Anna. The whole class laughed at Anna. Anna hadn't expected anyone to laugh at her. Suddenly Anna felt as small as a mouse and wanted to hide. Then she thought of the earth angel and her special place, and how important they both were to her. Once again, Anna felt strong and determined.

"You'll see," said Anna. "She's real. And real big too."

Anna ran to her special place after school, and the other kids ran after her. Anna saw the earth angel and sat down beside her. When the other kids saw the earth angel, they all ran home scared, except for Pria and Alexander, who hid behind the trees and watched.

"I'm very sorry," said Anna. "I guess they won't be cleaning up their mess after all. But at least they won't be back to make any more mess."

The earth angel smiled faintly at Anna. "I never wanted them to go away," she said sweetly. "They are all welcome to stay, but they must clean up the mess they've made of my home."

Pria looked at Alexander. Alexander looked at Pria. They both ran home. Anna and the earth angel sat in silence for a long time, looking over the hillside. They felt saddened by the events yet content to keep each other company.

CLANG! Anna heard a noise that startled her. She turned around to see Pria and Alexander holding shovels.

"Oh no you don't," said Anna, jumping to her feet, hands on her hips.

"We're not here to dig more trails," said Alexander. "We're here to clean up the mess."

Then more kids arrived over the hilltop. In fact, Anna's whole class returned, rakes and shovels in hand. Everyone worked on the trails. They filled the holes. They removed the log ramps. They smoothed the dirt.

"We're sorry about the flowers," said Pria to the earth angel. "We fixed the trail, but we can't fix the flowers."

"That's alright," replied the earth angel. "Nature will take care of that for you, if you leave her to her work."

That night Anna lay in bed, her arms folded behind her head, staring out her window at the stars and thinking about the earth angel. The earth angel lay at the top of the hill on her grassy bed, her wings folded behind her head, staring at the stars and thinking about Anna. This time Anna's heart was not heavy, but happy. This time the earth angel was at peace. And both fell asleep with smiles on their faces.

Winter came and laid its blanket of white across the hillside. Anna was busy with schoolwork and because the winter was even colder than usual, kids stayed indoors for most of the season.

But the earth angel was right. In spring, crocuses, new grasses, harebells and brown-eyed Susans shot up through the soil. The butterflies and ladybugs returned, and so did Anna. She would sit there as she used to and she would journal or sketch with her pencil.

And now she wasn't alone. All the kids came. Everyone enjoyed Anna's special place. Parents removed the barbed wire and created a proper entry to the hilltop: a wooden archway flanked by milkweed, which the butterflies loved. When Anna came to visit, she would always bow to the butterflies and she would always bow to the archway.

Very soon, it became a special place for the whole neighborhood. Anna was happy to share it. Children came to paint pictures of the prairie crocuses or watch the busy bugs. Adults came to hear wonderful stories told by the earth angel. They even came to play hide and seek...

but the earth angel's wings always gave her away.

The End

25

Acknowledgments

Anna's first adventure could not have happened without the loving support of family and friends:

Mom and Dad	Dan & Melodie Belich
Lynn & Earl Moker	Pat & Bob Wescott
Lisa Turner	Dawn & John Baisley
Emma Barry	Cindy Rankine Drummond
Cara Fitzgerald	Juli Alderson
Tammy Olson	Judith Caron
Rob and Andrea Brabec	my sister, Carol

and the many more who support Anna and me.

Special thanks to Pam and Brice Lefebvre!

Thank you to John Breeze for making me believe I could publish this book, and helping me navigate the world of self-publishing.

Thank you to Irene Naested for making me believe I could paint, and for introducing me to John Breeze.

I also acknowledge the caretakers of the special place in Calgary that I call home; place of Two-Toed Pond, of orange butterflies, thin-legged spiders, harebells and brown-eyed Susans, tall trees and even taller earth angels. Thank you to our Blackfoot, Stoney/Nakoda, and Tsuu T'ina neighbors for your care of these ancestral lands. May we all be caretakers of this magical place.

- Stephanie

About the Author

Stephanie Hrehirchuk lives in Calgary, Alberta, where she reads books with her daughter, learns how to use technology from her son, plays gin rummy with her husband, and writes about the world outside her door and inside her imagination. Anna and the Earth Angel is Stephanie's first children's book.